NETTLE FARM

WOODS

TURN BACK

KEEP OUT!

MOUSE MOUNTAIN

GREAT HAWTHORN

NUT TOWER

SECRET LOCH

OW STURE

PINE HILL

OLD MILL BRIDGE

OTTER POOL.

Best wishes,

Horace
and the
Haggis Hunter

SALLY MAGNUSSON

Illustrated by Norman Stone

BLACK & WHITE PUBLISHING

First published 2012
by Black & White Publishing Ltd
29 Ocean Drive, Edinburgh EH6 6JL

1 3 5 7 9 10 8 6 4 2   12 13 14 15

ISBN: 978 1 84502 436 9

Designed by Richard Budd Design
Reprographics by syntax21.co.uk
Printed and bound in Poland by
www.hussarbooks.pl

A SECRET MESSAGE
FOR READERS

Ask a grown-up 'What is a haggis?' and this is what they will tell you.

A haggis, they will say, is a dish made from the mashed insides of a sheep. Scots like eating it on the birthday of their great poet, Robert Burns, who wrote a poem about how it gushes out of the bag like a warm, wet pudding.

Yes, I know. Yuk.

But what would *you* say if I told you that the haggis is an animal belonging to a species as ancient as the unicorn, or the centaur, or the mighty griffin? Only smaller and fatter and, let's face it, not so mighty.

What would you say if I told you that greedy haggis hunters have snatched so many haggises to boil for dinner that there are only a few left on the face of the earth?

Perhaps you can imagine what it would feel like to be a lone haggis on the run from those hunters. He would need friends, wouldn't he? He would need animals to protect him, but also human friends to keep his whereabouts secret from the enemy. He would need you.

So, let the grown-ups believe their own story if they want to. I am going to tell you a better one. And once you have read it, please remember to keep our secret safe – or this timid endangered species may be lost forever.

The Author

1

A lean, hungry-looking fox crept out from behind the trees. He padded softly towards the plump creature lying asleep beside a tartan bag. His eyes gleamed.

Horace did not stir.

He had been running all day, from the moment the hunters arrived at his home while he was fixing his hair that morning. They had crept across the moor and swooped down on his mother as she collected heather outside their burrow.

'Run, Horace,' she had screamed. 'Run as far as you can. Run for your life.' No time for a goodbye. He had stuffed his hair gel into his pouch and grabbed his bagpipes. Then he had scurried away, trying not to hear his mother's squeals as the net closed over her head.

By the time Horace could run no more he was a long way from home. He lay down on the bank of a bubbling stream and fell asleep.

The fox peered at him in astonishment. What on earth was this creature? An overweight hare? A furry chicken with gelled hair?

And that nose.

'You could play a tune on that snout,' he whispered.

'Whatever he is, he looks exhausted,' a lighter, squeakier voice whispered back.

The fox sniffed.

'Well, Martha, he's got plenty of meat on him for such a little thing. If I wasn't a vegetarian . . . '

'But you *are* a vegetarian, Ferdy,' retorted his companion.

The fox glared at the little mouse. She ignored him.

'And if you ever feel like changing your habits, please start with that nasty cat up at Nettle Farm and not this . . . this . . . '

She hopped on to Horace's face and pattered across it, swishing her tail over his eyes and tickling his nose to wake him up.

'Excuse me, sir, but what exactly are you?'

Horace opened an eye. He sat up and rubbed his itchy nose. It played a note. PARP!

Martha was blown into the air and landed on Horace's soft round stomach.

He stared at the tiny field-mouse. She was wearing a bud of yellow gorse between her ears and a stripy red sweetie wrapper on her tail.

'Hello,' she fluttered. 'My name's Martha Mouse. And this is my friend Ferdy.'

Horace nearly passed out with shock. A fox! Great-Aunt Beryl had gone that way only last summer.

'Ferdinand Fox at your service,' boomed the animal importantly. 'And who might you be?'

Horace opened his mouth, but nothing came out.

'Don't worry. Ferdy won't harm you,' Martha soothed, pattering around his middle and peeking into his velvety pouch. 'He's got a heart of gold really. Eats flowers and rescues chickens in his spare time. Now, please, tell us who you are.'

'I'm Horace.'

'Eh?' grunted Ferdy. 'You don't look much like a horse to me.'

'No, HORACE. After a famous writer in Roman times. My father thought a great name would rub off on me and help me do great things.' He sighed. 'I'm afraid I'm still waiting.'

Martha giggled. Ferdy snorted impatiently.

'But Horace who?' he barked. His long white teeth gleamed and Horace quaked. 'Come on, laddie, what's the rest of your name? Spit it out.'

Horace put a finger to his trumpet-like nose and another PARP blasted out proudly. Martha shot into the air again.

'Horace the Haggis,' he proclaimed grandly.

'A haggis!' Martha shrieked in delight as she landed. 'A haggis, Ferdy, a real haggis!'

She ran up and down Horace's stomach, squeaking non-stop in excitement.

'Doc Leaf told us about haggises. He's an owl, Horace, and he knows everything. He said they had more or less died out. And I said what a pity, why had they died out? And Doc said it was because they were all so stupid, they kept getting caught and I said . . . um . . . oops . . . '

Martha patted her yellow bud and looked embarrassed. Ferdy glared at her.

But Horace just smiled, a little sadly. He stood up and popped the mouse into his furry white pouch, where she found herself standing on a plastic tube of hair gel.

'I'm afraid the owl was right, Miss Mouse. We haggises may be good-looking' (now it was Ferdy's turn to smile) 'but we have never been very clever. Not clever enough to keep out of hunters' nets anyway.'

Martha was sure she saw tears glinting in his big eyes.

'And I don't have a home any more. I suppose that's not very smart either, is it?'

He blinked the tears away and Martha gave him a sympathetic pat.

'Anyway,' Horace went on quickly, 'please could you tell me where I am and where I might get a spot of heather for supper? I'm very peckish.'

'Now, that's where I can help you,' said Ferdy, bustling forward. Horace quickly took a step back.

'You're in Acre Valley, a good class of neighbourhood on the whole. Away over there is the Secret Loch. My friend Professor Nut lives that way. He's designing me a mechanical root-plucker at the moment.'

'What's a . . . ?' Horace began. But the fox was rushing on.

'My own fine residence is further along the bank.' He pointed across the valley. 'Dun Foxin'. You must come for dinner.'

Martha rolled her eyes at Horace.

'And my friend the Major has his place not far from here. Excellent chap. In fact, there's an empty rabbit-hole down his way which might serve you as a burrow.'

'And, er, heather?' asked Horace. His tummy really was very empty.

'Oh yes, plenty of heather, although I prefer something with more flavour myself. The daffodils are very tasty at the moment. My chef

7

Horace and the Haggis Hunter

Dijon – a most talented young robin – is rustling me up a daffodil and wild garlic casserole as we speak.'

Ferdy licked his lips and Horace shuddered.

'As for heather, the very best of it is right up there, near the farm. But I advise you to stay well away from there, Horace. You don't want to mess with Angus McPhee.'

Horace froze. In fact, he actually stopped breathing for a moment. His stomach flipped over.

'What was that name?' he stuttered.

'McPhee,' said Martha. 'Angus McPhee, the farmer. Horrible man. Wounded Daphne Deer

with his shotgun last week. And he's got
a really deadly cat – The Cat With No
Name, we call her – who has personally
put paid to 327 of my relatives on
Mouse Mountain.'

Martha sniffled. 'She got one of
us just yesterday. Uncle Martin didn't
stand a chance. McPhee lets that cat
off with murder.'

Horace's legs felt so wobbly that
he had to sit down again.

'I know about Angus McPhee,' he sighed.
'My mother said he was chief of the haggis
hunters, the worst of the lot. She said there was
no-one in the whole country who could sniff out
a haggis like Angus McPhee.'

He groaned. 'And I've managed to run
straight to his doorstep.'

Martha and Ferdy stared at him, horrified.

'I told you haggises weren't very clever,'
Horace said glumly.

2

Next day Horace squeezed out of the rabbit
burrow into a sun-splashed spring morning.
Whipping out the tube of gel, he primped his
hair into a tuft of gleaming spikes and admired
himself in a puddle.

Then he settled the tartan bag on his chest,
puffed out his cheeks and gave a great blow into
one of the pipes. As the bag filled with air, the
peace of Acre Valley was shattered by a screech
like an animal in the most dreadful pain.

A large owl with a stethoscope around his
neck shot out of an oak tree and flapped away
urgently. The ground near Horace began to
tremble.

Horace blew again. This time his fingers
whisked over the holes in the lower pipe and
a tune emerged. 'Lament for a Lost Haggis'
reminded him of his mother.

Oh dear, he could feel tears welling up again. Time to play something happier.

A clod of earth shot into the air, then another. Horace was still too busy to notice. He was striding up and down the bank of the burn, puffing air and squeezing the bag with his arm, fingers flying.

Another spray of soil. This one nearly hit Horace in the eye and he stopped playing. What on earth was going on?

At that moment a steel helmet and a pair of spectacles burst out of the ground, followed by a stout body in a military jacket.

'Right men, hurry up – you heard the air-raid siren,' rasped a military voice. 'This is an emergency.'

Two more animals heaved themselves out of the hole and stood blinking in the sunlight.

Horace coughed politely. The leader swung around so fast that his glasses fell off. He shoved them back on and stood staring in astonishment.

'Courage, men,' he barked at last. 'This is obviously an alien invasion. I will attempt to parley with the enemy.'

He strode forward, brandishing a tiny twig.

'My name is Major Mole,' he said, chest swelling with pride. 'You see beside me the valiant members of the Mole Patrol, defenders of the realm of Acre Valley.'

'Pleased to meet you, Major,' said Horace cheerfully. 'Ferdy said I might bump into you.'

'Oh, you know Ferdinand?' said the mole, taken aback. His stick wavered.

'Yes, I do,' said Horace.

'But aren't you an alien invader?'

'No, I'm a haggis,' Horace said, and waited for a reaction.

Major Mole looked blank. Horace tried again.

'You know, the ancient race who have walked the earth since the beginning of time . . . or thereabouts. There are loads of legends about us. Mind you, some are plain silly – like saying we have three legs and run around in circles. Three legs, I ask you!'

'Well, I've never heard of you,' grunted the

Horace and the Haggis Hunter

Major. 'There have certainly never been any, what do you call 'em, haggises, in these parts, or we in the Underground Services would have heard about it.'

The mole leaned closer, catching his glasses as they toppled off again.

'But what was that siren a few minutes ago? Nearly frightened the wits out of my men, I can tell you.'

Horace grinned. 'Oh, that was my bagpipes. They belonged to my father. I'm just learning. I can play you another tune if you like.'

'Good gracious, no,' said the Major hurriedly. 'I have to be getting along for a bit of shut-eye. A pleasure to meet you, boy. Tally ho, men.'

Major Mole marched briskly back to the mound of earth, muttering to the sergeant that any friend of Ferdinand Fox's was a friend of his but this haggis was a rum fellow and no mistake.

Horace grinned to himself. He was starting to like these Acre Valley animals. How he wished he could stay and get to know them.

But there was no chance of staying. No chance at all. How could he live so close to a man who wanted to boil him for dinner? No, Horace knew he had to get as far from Angus McPhee as he possibly could.

He would leave Acre Valley right away – just as soon as he had found himself some breakfast.

3

'Well, good morning, gorgeous. It's not often I meet such a handsome stranger in Acre Valley.'

A sleekly-groomed cat was looking Horace up and down from beneath a big horse chestnut tree.

'I like your hair,' purred the cat, sliding closer. 'I always admire a bit of style.'

'Do you really?' Horace beamed. He fingered his rock-hard locks, trying, without success, to look modest. 'Actually I'm on the hunt for heather. You don't know where I can find some, do you?'

'So you like eating heather?' replied the cat in a slinky, musical voice.

'You bet,' chuckled Horace. 'I'm a haggis, you know. We can't get enough of it.'

The cat's eyes narrowed.

'So you're a haggis, are you? Well, well. I know someone who would be very pleased to meet a haggis.'

Horace patted his hair again and looked pleased.

'I'll take you to meet him, shall I?' the cat offered silkily. 'My friend lives near the juiciest heather in the whole valley. Come with me, you hunky haggis.'

So off they set, Horace and the cat, up the sloping side of the valley.

Horace was so busy explaining why he preferred gel to wax for his hair that he failed to spot a wisp of chimney smoke curling into the sky behind the hill. It was a very, very dangerous clue to miss.

From high in the tree the sound of cackling laughter followed them on their way.

4

Martha and Ferdy were wandering along the bank of the burn, looking for Horace.

'Maybe he's run away,' said Martha gloomily from her perch on Ferdy's head. 'He sounded very scared when you mentioned Farmer McPhee.'

Suddenly the fox stopped in his tracks. 'Hey,' he cried, 'isn't that Horace's funny bag?' He pointed to a patch of tartan in the grass. 'But where is he?'

'Can I be of assistance?' interrupted a glossy black bird from a nearby branch. He regarded them with dancing eyes.

'Well, I suppose the services of the biggest gossip in Acre Valley might come in useful,' harrumphed Ferdy.

'Me? Gossip? Darlings, as if! Mind you, did you hear what Professor Nut is up to this morning? He's invented this machine which he claims can change dandelions into . . . '

'Ronald, this is serious,' squeaked Martha. 'We're looking for a friend, a funny little round guy.'

'Rather vain?' Ronald butted in. 'Bit dim? Likes heather?'

'Yes, yes, that's him. Have you met him?'

'No,' said Ronald airily.

'Come on, Rook,' Ferdy growled, taking a threatening step towards the branch. 'If you know where Horace is, say so at once.'

Ronald Rook folded his feathers huffily. 'Well, as it happens, I did overhear a conversation under my tree. Not that I'm in the habit of, as it were, leavesdropping.'

'Of course not,' Martha tittered.

'Anyway I believe your friend may have headed up the hill with a certain cat.' The bird gave a throaty chuckle. 'The pair of them seemed to be getting on very well,' he winked, 'if you see what I mean.'

Martha and Ferdy looked thunderstruck.

'The Cat!' Martha squealed. 'She'll take him straight to Angus McPhee.'

Ferdy wheeled round and gazed up the hill. Horace would be there by now. They would never make it in time to save him.

Ronald's eyes were glinting with interest. 'Is there some problem I could assist with?'

'No, no. No problem at all,' sniffed Martha bitterly. 'Just a poor haggis being led to his death by the cruellest cat in Acre Valley history.'

'A haggis. So that's what he is,' mused Ronald. 'I did wonder.'

Martha was already bouncing impatiently on Ferdy's head.

'Come on, Ferdy, we're wasting time,' she shouted into his ear.

'Hold tight, then, Martha,' said the fox grimly. 'This will be fast.'

Ferdy sped off towards the hill with his bushy red tail streaming behind and Martha clinging on for dear life. Ronald Rook watched them go.

He had an idea.

5

Stacey Magpie was sitting in her nest near Nettle Farm, painting her nails. A brand new mobile phone lay beside her. To her annoyance it bleeped just as she started on her last claw.

'Oh, give Twitter a rest, Trace,' she muttered.

She carried on until the talon was a gleaming Putrid Pink, then tapped a button with her beak and read the tweet from her best friend Tracey.

T **Tracey Magpie** @TraceEmag
@StaceEmag McPhee on warpath. Ronald Rook says cre8 diversion. #Haggis4dinner

'Wow,' Stacey breathed. 'Work to do.'

With an admiring glance at her nails, she flew off.

22

6

Horace was in haggis heaven. Before nipping off to fetch her friend, the cat had led him to the thickest, springiest cushion of heather he had ever sunk his teeth into. It grew right in the corner of the top field, enclosed by a fence and a hedge of prickly yellow gorse.

Now he heard her purring to a halt behind him again.

'Hi,' he murmured without looking up, his mouth full. 'Thanks for this. It really is . . . ' (he burped and turned it into a cough) 'delicious. Did you find your friend?'

The cat said nothing.

Horace stopped chomping. He was not usually much good at sensing danger, but her silence gave him a prickly feeling at the back of his neck. Slowly, fearfully, he looked around.

The sight that met his eyes made his heart lurch so violently he thought he would faint.

Stepping quietly across the field towards him was a heavy man in a huge pair of black boots. He was carrying a long pole. And at the end of the pole hung . . .

A NET.

Horace saw it coming towards him. Too terrified to move, he felt its shadow over him. He knew this was the end and he shut his eyes to await his fate.

But then, all of a sudden, something streaked from the sky in a flutter of black and white feathers. Before the man knew what had hit him, a set of vivid pink talons was clawing ferociously at his face.

'Ow!' roared Angus McPhee, clutching his veiny red nose. 'Ow, ow, ow!'

'So much for my lovely nails,' muttered Stacey Magpie, tweaking even harder.

In desperation the farmer tugged the net off Horace. He swung it round and round to try and beat the bird off. Stacey clung on grimly.

Now this, of course, should have been Horace's moment to escape. Unfortunately, being Horace, he still had his eyes shut.

'Chase the magpie, Cat!' yelled the farmer, throwing his tormentor off at last. 'I'll get the haggis this time.'

'OH NO YOU WON'T!' snarled a familiar voice.

Panting from his fastest run ever to the top of Acre Valley, Ferdy the Fox leaped at McPhee. His jaws snapped hard.

The bellow of rage shocked even Horace into opening his eyes.

The farmer was clutching his bottom. His trousers were hanging off, revealing a large pair of underpants decorated with tulips. He was hopping with pain and fury.

Spitting out a piece of torn trouser, Ferdy placed himself between the farmer and the quivering haggis.

'Now, Horace!' roared Ferdy. 'Run for it!'

Horace tried to move. But have you ever tried a fast getaway on an over-full stomach?

He fell flat on his face.

'Going somewhere, handsome?' hissed a menacing voice. The cat was advancing on him now, with hackles raised and cold eyes.

'Not so fast, ugly,' taunted another voice, a high, squeaky, brave little voice. 'You leave my friend alone, you sly, mean, cruel, vile, vicious, horrible mouse-killer. You disgusting, smelly, stinky toilet-brush of a farmer-lover. You pathetic squirt of a haggis-trapper. You cowardly . . . ooh dear, Ferdy, help, she's coming.'

The cat lunged at Martha, slashing at her with a sharp claw and just missing the sweetie paper. The pair tore across the field.

'Help, Ferdy!' Martha squeaked as she ran.

The fox turned towards her. But as he did, the farmer grabbed a spade and whacked him hard on the head. Martha screamed. Ferdy collapsed and lay still.

'Martha, quick, come here,' Horace called. Sobbing, the mouse raced over and leaped into his pouch.

At that moment Horace felt something whisk through the air. He put his arms out and felt netting. The haggis hunter had him at last.

7

There is only one way to escape if you are trapped inside a net. Only one possible way out. Horace could not imagine it, but perhaps you can?

'Forward, men,' came a muffled whisper from under the ground. 'We're on the front line now. Silence in the ranks.'

McPhee had placed one giant boot on the end of the pole to trap Horace fast while he struggled with his sagging trousers. He was so busy trying to cover up his tulip underpants that he did not see a fountain of earth spraying up silently inside the net and a snout nosing into the sunshine right next to his prey.

Horace did, though.

'Major Mole!' he gasped.

'Underground intelligence, my boy – you can't beat it,' said the Major, brushing some earth off his glasses. 'Quick. We've made you a tunnel. Down you go.'

Horace dived headfirst into the hole. Two pairs of furry arms hauled him from below and the Major shoved from above. Oh dear, why had he eaten so much heather? The soil pressed tight around his stomach and he felt sick.

Byoing. Byoing. The Major was jumping on him now.

'Ouch,' yelled Horace. He felt like a trampoline.

Pulling in every muscle, he shot through the hole at last. As he picked himself up below, an indignant squeak came from his pouch.

'Would you please let me out of here? I'm feeling very squashed.'

'It's all right, Martha. We're safe now,' Horace said. 'I just wish I could say the same for poor Ferdy.'

He looked back up at the gaping hole. 'And where is the Major?'

At that moment a howl of terrible anger echoed down the tunnel and a furious face blocked out the daylight. McPhee had discovered he was gone.

Down the hole plunged an arm. A great hand reached for Horace in the darkness.

33

8

Above ground Major Mole was facing the enemy alone. He waved his trusty twig at McPhee's enormous backside.

'Turn round and fight, you big bahookie,' he commanded. 'My comrade Ferdinand will not die in vain.'

The mole did not notice a shadow falling across him – a shadow with pointy ears.

'Got you, you interfering pest!' hissed the cat, raising her polished claws to strike.

'I wouldn't do that if I were you,' came a low voice behind her. It was Ferdy, blood-splattered and shaky but very much alive.

The cat managed a nervous sneer. 'You!

You couldn't catch a one-legged duckling, you flower-eating freak.'

Ferdy bared his teeth and growled, suddenly looking incredibly fierce.

'OK, OK, keep your foxy fur on,' muttered the cat, backing away. Then she turned and sped off as fast as her paws would carry her.

As she left, another ear-splitting roar of rage sounded across the hillside.

'C-A-A-T! COME BACK HERE! YOU LET MY HAGGIS ESCAPE! WAIT TILL I CATCH YOU! NO DINNER FOR CAT!!!'

Angus McPhee was staggering home to the farm, his empty hands covered in mud, the net limp at his side.

9

Back in her nest Stacey Magpie smoothed her ruffled feathers and frowned at her nails. Just as she thought – smudged. She would have to varnish them all over again.

Never mind. It had been worth it to save that haggis. What an odd creature. She had never seen anything like him in her life.

And good for Trace. These smartphones she picked up the other day were coming in handy. Fun, too. The Angry Birds game was a laugh.

Stacey pecked the Twitter icon and tweeted a message:

S **Stacey Magpie** @StaceEmag
@TraceEmag Diversion cre8d. That haggis looks kinda cuddly lol. Wot u up 2 2nite? #Domynails?

36

10

Horace sat outside the burrow among his new friends, absent-mindedly playing a ballad on his nose. He was thinking about what he had to tell them. He wondered if he was brave enough to say it.

Ferdy was lying under a tree munching a daffodil, while a large owl dabbed at a wound on his head.

'Stay still, Ferdinand,' Doc Leaf was grumbling. 'I need to make sure this cut is clean.'

Ferdy was paying more attention to a plump robin taking orders for lunch.

'We are a little early for ze baked bluebell, *mon ami**,' Dijon was twittering, 'but cream of hawthorn is just coming into season.'

Meanwhile Major Mole was explaining his plans for an air strike on the farm to a squirrel in gigantic spectacles.

* mon ami = my friend. Dijon never forgets he trained as a chef in France.

'You see, Professor,' he was saying earnestly, 'if you could just provide me with some jet propulsion, I could lead an attack from the air. Our rooks and magpies are a fine fighting force.'

Professor Nut seemed to be trying to change the subject.

Horace looked around with a heavy heart. How was he going to tell them? He cleared his throat.

'I'm afraid I have to go,' he said loudly.

Everyone stopped talking at once and looked at him.

'Go?' said Ferdy. 'Go where? You've just arrived.'

'I don't know where. But I can't stay here. I'll . . . I'll . . . just make life dangerous for all of you.'

'Nonsense,' boomed a deep voice.

Abandoning his patient, the owl swooped over to Horace.

'I don't believe we've met yet. Doctor Wesley Leaf is the name,' he said, peering at

Horace with eyes as large as plates.

'Let me tell you, young lad, that you are welcome here in Acre Valley. You come from a fine race. None too bright, any of you, but kind and loyal. You stay and we'll all look out for you.'

'Mole Patrol reporting for duty,' saluted the Major.

'Quite right, Major,' said the owl. 'By the way, I think you'll find you are standing on your glasses.'

Major Mole peered anxiously at his feet and everyone laughed. Horace sighed.

'Oh, I wish I could stay. But I know those haggis hunters. Angus McPhee will never give up. Never.'

'And neither will we,' piped a little voice. Martha ran over to Horace, scampered up his leg and popped into his pouch.

'We'll help you, Horace,' she squeaked. 'Whatever happens in the future, we'll be with you. Won't we, Ferdy?'

The fox nodded gravely. 'We won the Battle

of Nettle Farm by sticking together. Make this your home, Horace, and that's what we'll keep doing.'

Horace looked at them all, hardly daring to believe it. They wanted him. His heart felt as if it would burst with happiness.

'All right,' he said, grinning from ear to ear, 'I'll stay.'

'Hooray for Horace,' shouted Ferdy, so enthusiastically that he choked on his daffodil. The others joined him in a deafening cheer.

Tracey Magpie tweeted the news on her phone right away. Stacey snapped a photo of Horace on hers. Ronald Rook began cawing the story to the rest of the valley at the top of his voice.

Horace reached into his burrow and pulled something out.

'I know just how to celebrate,' he declared happily.

His friends looked at each other in gravest alarm, panic in every eye.

'Sound the retreat!' roared the Major.

Horace and the Haggis Hunter

Doc Leaf took off like a rocket. Poor Dijon disappeared by mistake down a mole-hill.

'A tune on the bagpipes, anyone?' said Horace the Haggis.

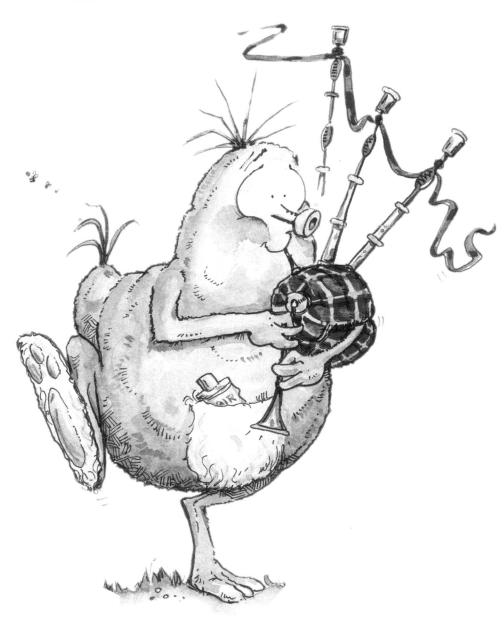

The End

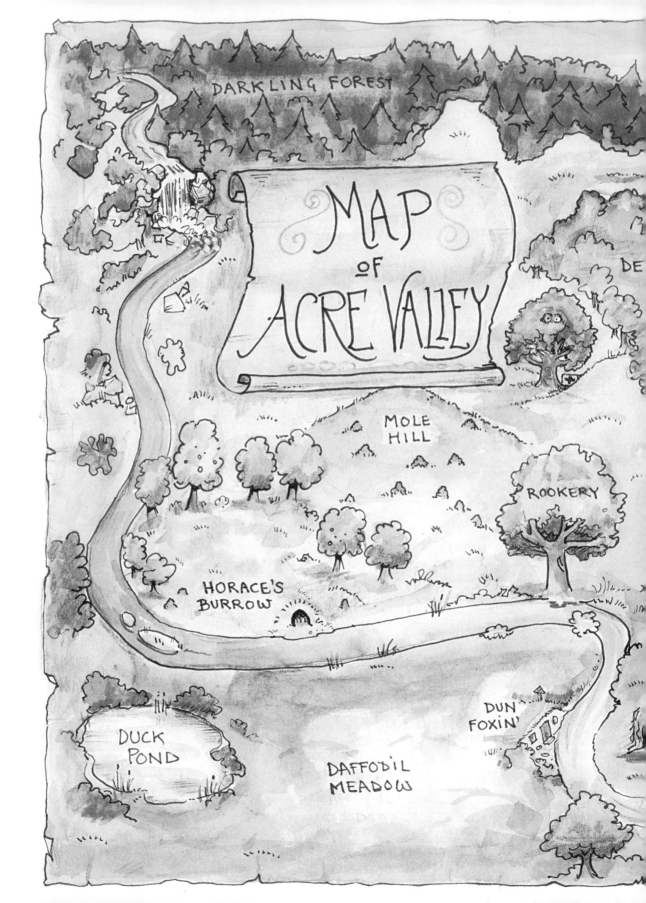